Also by Claude Clément
The Painter and the Wild Swans
Musician from the Darkness

Also illustrated by John Howe
Jack and the Beanstalk
Rip Van Winkle

First English Language Edition

First published in Belgium by Editions Duculot

ISBN 0-316-14741-9

Library of Congress Cataloging-in-Publication
information is available.

10 9 8 7 6 5 4 3 2 1

Printed in Belgium

WRITTEN BY CLAUDE CLÉMENT

ILLUSTRATED BY JOHN HOWE

THE MAN WHO LIT THE STARS

LITTLE, BROWN AND COMPANY   Boston   Toronto   London

He was a man with no belongings,
no family, no hearth to welcome him
home, a vagabond from nowhere with
no destination. On one shoulder, he
carried a tawny leather bag; on the
other, a ladder.

The thin voice of the wind
whispered in his ear and nipped at his
heels, keeping pace with his step. On
his lonely road, he had only the birds
for company.

Late one day, weariness and chance led him to a small village. There, all was still. The damp mist pressed heavily against the dark windows of the houses.

A lone ragged child sat on a weathered bench. He looked as if he were waiting for someone. Absently, he filled his shabby cap with small black-and-white pebbles. He spoke to no one.

The stranger looked at the boy as if he recognized him. But he did not pause.

The ragged boy emptied his cap of stones and on impulse, rose to follow the man.

They walked, one behind the other, until they reached the village square. Two woodcutters squatted on the damp ground, worn ivory dice in their large hands. Their hard eyes narrowed when the vagabond asked where he might find food and drink. One grunted in a rough voice, "What is your job, wanderer? Chimney sweep? If you want food and drink, you'll have to work for it!"

The stranger replied, "I am not a chimney sweep. I polish the stars."

Harsh laughter greeted the stranger. But the men soon grew angry as the stranger stood silent in the face of their laughter. Their mocking cries rang out under the low sky: "Fool! You're making fun of us, you buffoon! We want nothing to do with crazy vagabonds like you. Go and look for food somewhere else!"

The stranger turned and left without a word. A short way behind, the boy followed.

In the middle of a vast field, the wanderer halted. The birds had gone ahead and were waiting for him there, squabbling over a few fallen grains of wheat.

The stranger took the heavy ladder off his weary shoulder and slowly raised it upright against the sky. The boy strained to see the topmost rungs, but they were lost among the dark clouds.

The man began to climb his
ladder, the fluttering wings of the
birds surrounding him. Halfway up, he
paused to catch his breath and watch
the night fall on the distant horizon.
The wind tugged at his hair and cloak.
One by one, his winged companions
abandoned him to search for their
night's lodgings in the bushes far
below. One lone bird continued to
flutter about his hand.

Below, the child waited, watching.

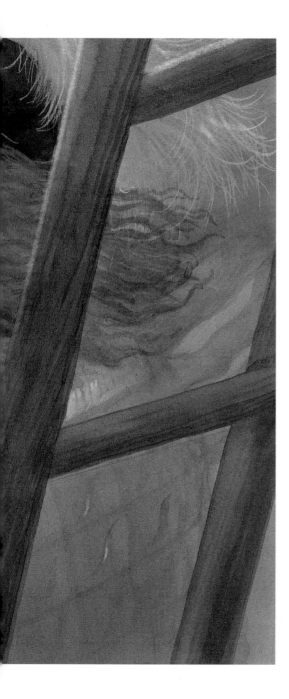

The climber softly cupped the frightened bird in his hand. When he opened his fingers, the wind plucked the bird away and led it in wide floating spirals toward the earth below. As the boy watched, the bird came to land in the stubble of the field.

As the man continued to climb into the darkened sky, the boy lost sight of him. The wind chilled him. Perhaps it was time to return home. Home to an empty corner of a deserted stable, where only a cold nest of straw awaited him.

He hesitated for a moment, then decided to stay. Surely the stranger would come down again. Who knew what he might bring back from his journey into the night sky?

Far above, the man reached the top of the ladder. The topmost rungs were propped against a dark, dull sphere. He drew a rag of rough cloth from his bag. Slowly, deliberately, he rubbed the dusty surface of the sphere. A faint glow began to light his face. The boy could now see the stranger through a tear in the ragged clouds, and he began to understand. Threadbare, homeless, and penniless though he may be, this mysterious stranger had the power to set the stars alight.

Suddenly, the boy wanted to help the stranger. He approached the ladder and began to climb. Soon he was far above the ground. The wind pried at his tired fingers and pinched his face. His clothes snapped like a flag in a gale. Several times he halted, breathless.

Courage and hope were swept away like leaves on a winter storm. Only one thing spurred him on: the thought of the man high above, slowly, painstakingly bringing light to the night of the world.

When at last the boy reached the top, the stranger offered him an outstretched hand. The ragged boy took off his cap and, side by side, the two polished the star.

Below, the two woodcutters trudged home across the deserted field. Suddenly, one halted and exclaimed, "Look there! What is it? It looks like . . . a ladder!"

The other shrugged. "A ladder? In the middle of a field? Nothing to lean it on," he muttered. "It's nothing but a dead sapling." And without an upward glance, he seized his ax and struck.

The man and the boy, perched on the very top of the ladder, suddenly lost their balance. The rung slipped away beneath their feet. The boy was frightened, but his companion laughed. "Don't be afraid. There is nothing to fear. We will travel the skies together, from star to star, and soon the night sky will be filled with the light we've made! And those who know enough to gaze at the stars will have something beautiful to dream about."

The woodcutters gathered up the dry wood that they had cut.

"Look!" cried one, pointing to the sky.

"What's the matter?" snarled the other.

"Over there! A falling star!"

The stranger was never seen again in that gray, wet country. Nor was the boy who waited and spoke to no one. And now, on summer nights, they say that you can sometimes see a half-lit star shooting tirelessly across the deep, dark sky.